For Rachel Louisa
~ *J.W.*

For the St Agnes fishermen
and young friends
~ *N.R.*

Published in 1998 by Magi Publications
22 Manchester Street, London W 1 M 5 PG

Text © 1998 Judy Waite
Illustrations © 1998 Neil Reed

Judy Waite and Neil Reed have asserted their
rights to be identified as the author and illustrator
of this work under the Copyright, Designs and
Patents Act, 1988

Printed in Belgium by Proost NV, Turnhout

ISBN 1 85430 464 X

~ The ~
Storm Seal

Judy Waite
illustrated by Neil Reed

The weather was wild. Angry lightning scratched
across the grumbling sky. The waves heaved and
hurled, and in the exploding night,
pressed against giant grey rocks,
the seals were huddling.

By morning, the storm had faded.
The wind dropped to a shout, then a whisper.
Along the sand an old man was walking,
clearing rubbish. And as he searched carefully
between rags of seaweed, something stirred.

Tangled amongst the knots of an old fishing
line lay a tiny seal pup, barely breathing.
"Poor little thing," said the old man,
wrapping it gently
in his jersey.

A boy playing on the beach spotted the old man and ran towards him.
"It's Peter!" he cried, calling out to his friends.
"I think he's found something."
The retired sailor was well known in the village for rescuing hurt animals.

Peter put his finger to his lips as the children came
near. "Ssssh," he whispered gently. "Don't crowd
round. He needs lots of peace and quiet."
The children understood, and watched silently as
Peter carried his precious bundle up the steep path
to his home.

Peter made a place in the kitchen for the baby seal, and offered him fish soup from a bottle. But the little pup just closed his eyes and turned away. So Peter sat and stroked his head and sang to him softly all the songs he knew from his days at sea.

By evening the pup had taken his first, spluttering drink. And when the soup was gone, he sucked gently on Peter's hand for comfort, while the velvet night crept softly in through the windows.

Next morning, the little seal seemed brighter.

And as the days passed, he grew stronger still. Soon he had lost his white baby fur, and was eating the fresh fish Peter tossed to him every morning.

He often followed Peter around, and when the days grew warmer, he played in the garden with the other animals.

Now that the seal was better, the children came to visit him. He rolled on his back and pawed them with his flipper, like a dog wanting a game.

More and more people came to visit the little seal. Peter was glad they were interested, but thankful, too, when the night came, and the two of them could enjoy the quiet for a while.

Then, one morning, Peter fell ill.
The doctor came, and ordered him to bed.
But Peter was anxious about all his animals.
"Don't worry," the doctor promised. "I'll arrange
for someone to help."

And he did. The local people were wonderful.
They shopped and they cleaned, they brushed and
they fed. Every day after school, the children came.
They helped with all the animals, but most of all,
they loved to help with the seal.

One day, the children brought a ball,
and taught the seal to balance it on his nose.
They dressed him up in sunglasses, a hat and
a scarf.

The seal looked funny in his new outfit,
but he didn't look much like a seal any more.

Upstairs, Peter was feeling better. He wondered
what all the noise was about. Slowly, he got up
and went downstairs.

Nobody noticed him as he stood in the doorway.
They were all too busy laughing at the seal.
"Oh no," said Peter, stepping forward. "Remember,
he's a wild animal. He might nip if he gets frightened.
And he's much too special for tricks and toys."
He knew now that he had something to get strong for.

Early each morning, Peter rowed out to sea.
He took the seal with him, and taught him how
to dive for food among silver flashes of fish.

And one morning, as the soft pink of sunrise still washed the sky, Peter saw something moving around the rocks. It was a great colony of seals.
One broke away from the others, and swam right up to the boat. Peter's seal stared hard at the stranger. "Don't worry," said Peter gently. "It's a friend."

The seal touched Peter lightly with his nose, then leapt into the water with a splash of sparkling silver. The other seal swam with him, nudging and nuzzling, then dived suddenly away.

Peter's seal swam back to the boat. "It's all right," said Peter. "It's time for you to go."
Then Peter's seal dived after his new friend, and the game began.

The two seals raced and chased, they rumbled
and tumbled, deep in the water under the boat.
And Peter rowed back to the shore through
the bright burst of morning.

On the beach the children were waiting.
They were worried about the seal.
"Look out to sea," said Peter, pointing.
"He's back where he belongs."

The children turned to where two black shapes
bobbed and splashed in the water.
"He has a friend already," said Peter, smiling.
"And see, it looks like they're laughing. It looks
like they're happy."
And, as they watched the seals slip away into the
distance, Peter and the children were happy, too.